World Record Mystery

Don't miss a single

Nancy Drew Clue Book:

Pool Party Puzzler

Last Lemonade Standing

A Star Witness

Big Top Flop

Movie Madness

Pets on Parade

Candy Kingdom Chaos

And coming soon:

Springtime Crime

Nancy Drew

* CLUE BOOK *

#8

World Record Mystery

BY CAROLYN KEENE * ILLUSTRATED BY PETER FRANCIS

Aladdin

NEW YORK   LONDON   TORONTO   SYDNEY   NEW DELHI

ALADDIN

An imprint of Simon & Schuster Children's Publishing Division
1230 Avenue of the Americas, New York, New York 10020
First Aladdin paperback edition October 2017
Text copyright © 2017 by Simon & Schuster, Inc.
Illustrations copyright © 2017 by Peter Francis
NANCY DREW, NANCY DREW CLUE BOOK, and colophons
are registered trademarks of Simon & Schuster, Inc.
Also available in an Aladdin hardcover edition.

For information about special discounts for bulk purchases, please contact Simon & Schuster
Special Sales at 1-866-506-1949 or business@simonandschuster.com.
The Simon & Schuster Speakers Bureau can bring authors to your live event.
For more information or to book an event contact the Simon & Schuster Speakers Bureau
at 1-866-248-3049 or visit our website at www.simonspeakers.com.
Series designed by Karina Granda
Book designed by Nina Simoneaux
The illustrations for this book were rendered digitally.
The text of this book was set in Adobe Garamond Pro.
Manufactured in the United States of America 0519 QVE
2 4 6 8 10 9 7 5 3
Library of Congress Control Number 2017943563
ISBN 978-1-4814-5836-8 (hc)
ISBN 978-1-4814-5835-1 (pbk)
ISBN 978-1-4814-5837-5 (eBook)

* CONTENTS *

Chapter

1

FOR THE RECORD!

"Go, Katie! Go, Katie!"

Nancy Drew and her best friends, Bess Marvin and George Fayne, joined the rest of the crowd at Starcade cheering for River Heights teen Katie McCabe as she spun across the electronic floor pad of the Dance-A-Thon video game. The local arcade was full of fans watching the gaming whiz practice her moves. Katie's feet flew over the lit-up squares, and she added arm movements to match the rhythm. In just a few hours, a judge from the Beamish Book of World Records would be there to record Katie's attempt to break the current high score!

"This is so exciting!" exclaimed Nancy.

"I hope by the time I'm sixteen *I* can dance like Katie," Bess said. She tried out a kick step and almost crashed into George.

Nancy laughed. "Good thing you have a few years to practice. I think you might need them."

Nancy and her friends were eight, and even though they didn't have dance moves like Katie, they were already experts at one thing: solving mysteries. Nancy, Bess, and George called themselves the Clue Crew.

George shook her head, causing her short dark hair to flop this way and that. "I know dancing takes a lot of athletic skill, but I'll take soccer over sashaying anytime."

George was the tomboy of their group. She and her cousin Bess were as different as night and day, but that didn't stop them from being as close as could be.

Bess pulled her blond hair into a ponytail and fastened it with a sparkly clip. "I just hope the judge hurries up and gets here."

Nancy laughed at her eager friend. "I hate to tell you, but I heard that the judge isn't scheduled to arrive for a couple of hours. That just means we have time to play some games of our own, if you want."

George led the way to the change machine that let them exchange their allowance money for game tokens. "How about some Skee-Ball to start?" she suggested. "It's my favorite."

The three girls took turns bowling at the Skee-Ball game. Bess got three balls into the tiny opening worth one hundred points and collected six tickets when the game ended.

"I'm saving up for the lava lamp I saw behind the prize counter," she said. "It will look super groovy in my room! And the base is pink—my favorite!"

"You'll need to win a lot more games to have enough tickets for a prize that big, Bess," Nancy said, handing her friend the three she'd scored.

"I have that same lava lamp in my arcade, and it costs seventy-five fewer tickets than here."

The girls turned around to find Christopher Finn, the owner of Gamespot, just behind them. His arcade was down the street and was another popular hangout spot for the kids in River Heights.

"Sorry to eavesdrop," Mr. Finn said, stuffing his hands in his pockets. "It's just so crowded in here, I couldn't help but stand close."

Nancy was jostled again, this time by a kid

racing past her to the photo booth. She grimaced. "That's okay, Mr. Finn. There *are* a ton of people in here today."

"Tell me about it," he replied. "My arcade's practically a ghost town this morning. Everyone would rather be here, cheering on Katie. I sure wish I had the Dance-A-Thon game at my place."

Mr. Finn hung his head and shuffled past the girls. Bess, Nancy, and George shared a sympathetic look, but it took only a few moments for them to get back in the mood to play.

The arcade was full of energy and sounds: bells, dings, chimes, laughter, and happy squeals!

Nancy was a pro with the giant padded hammer as she earned eight tickets at Whack-A-Worm. Next the girls climbed into plastic cars that moved them side to side and up and down as they raced each other on big screens in front of them. Bess and Nancy leaned into the racetrack turns while George yelled at her car to go, "Faster, faster!"

When they were done racing, Bess and George played against each other in air hockey. For two girls so different, their skills were well matched and the game ended in a tie score.

"Hmm, I know we said I'd play the winner, but how will we pick now?" Nancy asked, rubbing her chin.

"I'll play you, Nancy."

The girls spun around to see Michael Malone holding up a game token in his hand. Michael was in fourth grade and a close buddy of Ned Nickerson, one of Nancy's friends.

"Sure, Michael. I'll play you," Nancy said. "Are you any good?"

Michael held the token up to the sky and blew on it, before dropping it into the air hockey machine and pressing start.

"Not to brag too much, but I'm good at every game. I have the high score on three of the machines here."

He flipped the red puck in his hands before setting it onto the center of the table.

Chapter

2

OUT OF STEP

Bess put her hand on her hip. "Well, not to brag, but Nancy here is pretty good herself. And what was with that blowing-on-the-token thing?"

Michael smiled as he moved his mallet back and forth in front of his goal, blocking Nancy's attempt to shoot a goal. "That's for luck. It's just a thing I do whenever I put a token into a game. Must be working too, since I *do* hold all those high scores."

The puck landed on his side of the table, and

he aimed at Nancy's goal. With one hard *whack*, he sent the round piece of plastic right through the empty space she was guarding. George made a face as the scoreboard read 1–0.

"Well, you won't be holding any records on the Dance-A-Thon game, that's for sure. No one can beat Katie." George grabbed the puck from underneath the machine and returned it to the middle.

"That's true," Michael acknowledged. "She's really amazing at that one. I'm all left feet when it comes to dancing. But I do have another talent I'm hoping will earn me my own Beamish World Record."

He glanced up at George, and Nancy took advantage of his attention being off the game to send her puck flying at Michael's goal. She scored!

Bess and George jumped up and down. When they finished celebrating, Nancy asked, "Did you say you had your own world record in mind?"

Michael nodded, this time keeping his eyes firmly on the hockey game in progress. "That's right. I'm kind of worried, though. Earning a world record is a really long process. You have to contact a judge months and months ahead of time. Even then there's no guarantee one will come."

The puck went back and forth, back and forth across the surface.

"I was hoping the judge could watch me too," Michael continued, "but she'll only be in town for the afternoon. So there would only be time to watch Katie's attempt. It stinks. HEY!"

He yelped as a little girl came up behind him and covered his eyes.

"Guess who?" she asked.

Thwap! The puck slammed into Michael's goal. "No fair," he said as he pried the hands off his face. "I was distracted by my little sister!"

Nancy shrugged, but then she grinned. "Oh, all right. We won't count that goal." She turned to the girl standing next to Michael. "Hi, Caroline."

Caroline Malone waved at Nancy and ducked as her brother swatted at her. She quickly moved out of his reach and stood next to Bess.

"Oh, wow! Caroline, those are really awesome laces!" Bess said, pointing at Caroline's white sneakers. They sported glittery laces with tiny rhinestones sparkling along them. "Where did you get them?"

Caroline blushed and smiled. "I made them. If you want, I can make you a pair too. I have lots of supplies left over." She turned to Nancy and added, "You and George, too."

"Would you really? I'd love my own pair. I have the perfect sneakers for them!" Nancy exclaimed. "George, what about you?"

"No offense, Caroline, but rhinestones aren't really my thing," George said.

"Would it have to be laces?" Bess asked. "I have a purse strap I'd love to have decorated, if it's not too much work."

Caroline nodded. "Easy peasy! I can BeDazzle anything!"

Bess clapped. "I can even pay you for it. If you don't mind payment in game tokens, that is . . .

since I just spent the last of my allowance."

"Wow," Caroline breathed. "This is so cool!" She looked between the girls happily, until her brother tugged on her arm.

"C'mon, sis. I think I just got a great idea for getting the judge to make time for me!" He tossed his air hockey mallet at George. "Here. You can finish. Thanks for the game, Nancy."

Nancy, Bess, and George watched Michael and his sister disappear into the crowd.

"That was weird. He left mid-game," said Nancy.

George shrugged and plopped the puck into the center of the table. "Get ready to eat my dust, Nancy!"

A few minutes after Nancy had beaten George 10–8, the girls noticed a commotion over by the Dance-A-Thon machine.

"Do you think the judge is here?" Bess asked.

"Let's find out!" Nancy said, grabbing hold of her friends.

But when they got there, they saw a small

crowd surrounding Katie McCabe, who was wiping tears from her cheeks.

"What happened?" Nancy asked her classmate Deirdre. Nancy and Deirdre weren't always the best of friends, but Deirdre *was* always up on the latest gossip. Sure enough, she had her reporter's notebook out and was scribbling in it, taking notes for the blog post she was going to write about the day.

"Katie says she can't attempt the high score

today! Apparently, she took a break to get some water and switch the headband she's been practicing in for the lucky one she wears whenever she plays the game for top scores. But when she opened her bag, the headband was gone!"

Deirdre's eyes were sparkling the way they always did when she had juicy gossip to deliver. But then she looked over Nancy's shoulder and squeaked. "Oh! Gotta go! I snagged an interview with Max Bensen, the boy who currently holds the record Katie's trying to break, and I just spotted him! Bye!"

Deirdre rushed over to a teenage boy in baggy pants, wearing a baseball cap low over his eyes. She didn't even spare a backward glance at the three girls she'd left behind.

Nancy, Bess, and George exchanged a look. "Girls, do you know what this means?" Nancy asked. Before they could even speak, she answered herself.

"A mystery that needs solving. The Clue Crew is on it!"

Chapter

3

WITH ANY LUCK

Nancy and her friends had a notebook of their own. But instead of a place to compile news tidbits, like Deirdre's was, theirs was a Clue Book. They used it to write down all the suspects and clues as they solved their way through every mystery. It had never failed them before, and Nancy knew it wouldn't this time either.

"We have some information gathering to do, girls," she said to her friends, clicking her pen.

Nancy, Bess, and George glanced over at Katie

again. The star dancer, who always seemed so confident and happy on the dance pad, was anything but upbeat now.

"This is really bad," said Bess. "What if we can't find her lucky headband before the judge gets here? Michael made it sound like it was super hard to get the Beamish World Records people to come watch an attempt. This could be her one big chance!"

George chewed her lip before saying, "Yeah. We know we're the best junior detectives in River Heights. But are we the fastest?"

Nancy tucked her notebook under her arm and grabbed both her friends by the hands. "We won't be if we don't stop standing around and get to work. C'mon, let's start by talking to Katie."

They squeezed through the people surrounding Katie until they were standing next to the teenager. She wore knee-length black leggings underneath a hot-pink ballet tutu, paired with a tank top that read GRRRL POWER. Katie's hair had a matching streak of hot pink.

Bess sighed happily and whispered to George, "I love when someone owns her style."

George rolled her eyes and whispered back, "Headband, remember?"

Bess put a hand on her hip. "You don't have to remind me to think of accessories, George. Half the time I already am!"

Nancy cleared her throat. "Excuse me, Katie?"

Katie turned and looked at the girls. "Yes?" she asked, tucking a tissue underneath her eye and blotting her tears. "Sorry," she added, motioning to the tears. "I know it's just a video game, but this record means so much to me. And so does my lucky headband."

All three girls nodded in sympathy.

"We're hoping we can help you out. We specialize in solving mysteries like this," Nancy said, not bothering to hide the pride in her voice.

From behind her she heard, "They aren't lying. These girls are the best detectives around!"

The voice came from their classmate Quincy Taylor, from River Heights's Ghost Grabbers

Club. The girls had met Quincy when he'd thought the costume Nancy's dog Chocolate Chip had been wearing in the Howl-a-Ween Pet Parade might have been haunted by a ghost. The Clue Crew had been able to prove Chip's strange behavior had been caused by something way less creepy . . . and had earned a fan for life.

"Thanks for the vote of confidence, Quincy," Bess said.

Katie's tears were already drying, and while she wasn't quite smiling, her mouth turned up a little in one corner. "I'd love if you could help me!" But then it drooped again. "Except I don't really have much to give you in terms of clues. I was so in the zone during my practice round that I didn't pay any attention at all to my duffel bag until about five minutes ago, when I went searching for my lucky headband."

Nancy smiled. "That's okay. Maybe the bag itself will tell us something. Could you show us where it is?"

"Oh, and also describe the missing headband for us," added George.

"Yes, spare no detail on the fabulous accessories!" Beth piped in. George poked her in the side, and the next word out of Bess's mouth was a quiet "Ouch!"

Katie led the girls to a spot just to the left of the Dance-A-Thon game pad, where a pinball machine displaying an OUT OF ORDER sign cast a long shadow on the tile floor. A black duffel with a hot-pink handle poked out from underneath the game. It was open and the contents were jumbled, as if someone had been searching through them and hadn't bothered to return anything neatly to its place. It might have been Katie, who'd just been looking for the lost headband. Or, Nancy thought, maybe it was whoever had taken it.

"I keep my bag right under this pinball machine, so no one trips on it. It's my usual spot, and no one has ever bothered it before. I never imagined I had to even think about theft, especially since there's nothing in here anyone else would find valuable. Just a plain white headband, some fresh socks, and a handful of clean washcloths. I can get pretty hot when I'm dancing really hard, and the headband keeps any sweat from dripping in my eyes while I dance. If I can't see, I could miss a move, and even one misstep means my perfect score goes . . . bye-bye!" Katie made the fingers on her left hand waggle as she raised them, miming something flying away.

Beth shuddered. "That sounds like a lot of pressure."

Katie smiled. "It can be. But I love it. And once I'm in the groove, I feel like I could dance forever. It's getting into that groove that's the problem now. I need my headband for that!"

"What if we ran to my house and brought you one of my headbands to keep your hair out of your eyes?" Nancy suggested, but Katie shook her head sadly.

"I wish that would solve things, but I need *my* lucky headband to play. I know it might sound silly, but actually, a lot of athletes are superstitious. Some baseball players refuse to change their socks or shave their beards when they're on a winning streak."

George put in, "When I'm playing basketball, I always have to bounce the ball three times before shooting a free shot."

"Ooh, I read that Bettina Williams, the tennis star, does that. She bounces five times before her first serve, and twice before her second," Nancy added.

Katie nodded. "I really do believe my headband brings me luck. I can't imagine trying to break the world record without it. It just wouldn't work. I know it!"

Nancy touched Katie's arm. "We'll do our very best to find it, then. Can you describe it to us, please?"

"Sure. It's pretty basic, really. Just a loop of plain old white, stretchy fabric. About this thick—" Katie held up her fingers about an inch apart. "Really, it's nothing special . . . except to me."

As she talked, Katie tugged the duffel out from under the pinball machine and handed it to George. "Maybe you can find some clues in here, but I can't begin to imagine who would do something like this to me!"

Just then Katie's mom called over and motioned for Katie to come speak to Max Bensen, who must have finished his interview with Deirdre. Katie thanked the girls and rushed to Max. He gave her a sympathetic hug and pointed at the clock on the wall. Katie grimaced.

The girls did too. The judge would be there soon.

The Clue Crew didn't have any time to waste!

Chapter

4

THE CLUES IN THE BAG

George set the canvas duffel
bag on top of the out-of-service
pinball machine. The motion
made one of the tiny bells
inside the game ring. All
three girls began
to gently pull
items from the
bag, inspecting
each closely.

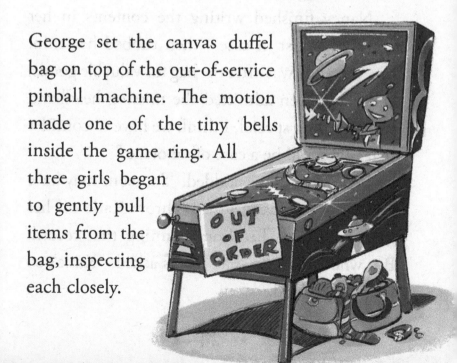

As Katie had mentioned, the contents of the bag consisted entirely of fluffy white washcloths—only a few of which were still folded—and three pairs of clean white socks. George held one pair up and shook gently, watching as a few pieces of pink glitter clinging to them floated off in the air. She set them down on the glass top of the pinball game.

"Well," she said, "Katie was right. I don't think we're going to get a lot of clues from this bag. It's exactly what she said: washcloths and socks. Not so interesting to thieves!"

Nancy finished writing the contents in her notebook—just in case—then rubbed her chin. "So, if no one was after the bag for valuable goods, and Katie even admitted the missing headband isn't anything special, I think we have to consider that this could be a case of sabotage."

Bess and George nodded. "Someone may have taken the headband just to throw Katie off her game and keep her from winning that record. But who would do that?" Bess asked. "Katie's so nice!" she added.

"She really is so sweet," Nancy agreed. She stared at the floor and then cocked her head to the left as she leaned in for a closer look at something she spied there. "Maybe the person didn't have anything against Katie herself. Maybe they just didn't want the record broken by *anyone*."

She bent down and picked up an arcade token and held it up for the other girls to see.

Bess's forehead wrinkled. "What does a token have to do with Katie's headband? Everyone here has those tokens in their pockets. Anyone could have dropped that."

Nancy turned the token over and said, "Everyone here has tokens from Starcade. But look!"

George peered at the token, then proclaimed, "This is a token for Gamespot!"

The tokens for the rival arcade up the street were silver, unlike Starcade's, which were a dark bronze color.

Nancy nodded. "Right. And Mr. Finn said

Gamespot has been pretty much a ghost town because he doesn't have the Dance-A-Thon game. If Katie wins the world record here, it would probably be really good for Starcade's business. And what's good for Starcade's business is bad for Gamespot's business! Plus, we know Mr. Finn was here. What if he took Katie's headband to keep her from winning?"

Bess took a step back and bumped against the pinball machine, which went *ding!* in return. "We have to find Mr. Finn!"

All three girls went up on tiptoes to search for the arcade owner in the crowd, but they couldn't spy him anywhere. They decided he must have returned to his own arcade.

Glancing at her watch, Nancy said, "Field trip time!"

The members of the Clue Crew rushed up the street to Gamespot.

When they arrived, the girls found a quiet arcade. Sure, there were a few people throwing basketballs into a hoop surrounded by netting on three sides, and several others clustered around a row of vintage video games with names like Space Invaders and Ms. Pac-Man, but it was far from the crowded scene at Starcade.

They spotted Mr. Finn easily. He was behind the counter, polishing the glass display that housed all the prizes customers could exchange their tickets for. He was sucking on a lollipop and carefully rubbing a spot on the glass, but he looked up when the girls approached.

"Hello, ladies. Twice in one day. You didn't want to stick around and watch the record-breaking attempt? Too crowded for you?"

George peered into the case of prizes and said, "It really *is* crowded there."

Mr. Finn took the green lollipop from his mouth and smiled. "Well, I'm happy to offer a quiet alternative if you're looking to play some games. But I have to warn you, if my plans work out, it won't be empty in here much longer."

"What do you mean?" Nancy asked.

Mr. Finn scratched his head with the hand that wasn't holding his lollipop. "When I bumped into you at Starcade, I wasn't that thrilled with all the customers they had, but as I walked back here, I realized something."

Bess propped an elbow on the counter. "What's that, Mr. Finn?"

She followed his eyes to her elbow and quickly stepped back. "Sorry!" she said, using her shirt to rub off the smudge mark her elbow had left on the just-cleaned glass.

Mr. Finn just laughed and waved off her sleeve, using his rag instead. "Seeing all those people at Starcade inspired me to make Gamespot even better. Instead of passing by the bank on my way here, I went in and applied for a loan to buy the new Surf City game. It lets players feel like they're really riding giant waves. I'm going to have a big contest to find someone who can beat its world record, with me as their sponsor. He or she can play as many free games of Surf City as it takes while training to be champion."

"I've always wanted to try surfing!" George declared.

Mr. Finn grinned. "Well, there you go, then. You can be my first champion-in-the-making." He popped his green lollipop back in his mouth and gestured at the case. "In the meantime, how about a free prize for three of my favorite customers?"

He held out plastic spider rings to each of the girls. They offered smiles and thanks as they accepted the gifts.

Nancy was just about to steer their conversation back to Katie and the missing headband, when George linked arms with the other girls and said, "Thanks again, Mr. Finn. Have a great afternoon!"

"Oh, I intend to. I'm going to plan out how to rearrange the games I have, so I can make room for Surf City!"

"Although—" Nancy began, but George gently tugged her and Bess away from the counter and out the door.

Chapter

KNOCK YOUR SOCKS OFF

"George, we barely started talking to him. Nancy was just working up to the good questions!" Bess said, nudging her cousin.

George held her hand out to admire her black spider ring and said casually, "Oh, don't worry. We got everything we need to eliminate him as a suspect."

Nancy and Bess turned to George in surprise. "We did?" Bess asked.

George nodded smugly. "He was sucking on a green lollipop."

Bess and Nancy stopped and stared at George like she was speaking a foreign language.

"What does a green lollipop have to do with anything?" Bess asked.

George shrugged. "He said he stopped at the bank between here and Starcade to apply for a loan. That would be River Heights Savings and Loan."

She pointed at the bank a few storefronts away from them. An elderly woman was just pushing through the door, busily unwrapping a lollipop. A *green* lollipop.

Nancy was beginning to see where George was going with this. "They give lollipops to all their customers."

George grinned. "Yup. And the tellers always

try to get the adults to take the green ones, since they have lots of them left over."

"Why's that?" asked Bess.

"Because every kid everywhere knows the red ones are the best flavor," George said. "Those are always the first to go!"

Bess nodded, impressed with George's detective skills. Nancy was too, even though she couldn't help adding, "I like the yellow ones."

Bess and George made *blech!* faces.

"So Mr. Finn was busy applying for his loan at the bank when Katie's headband went missing," Nancy said, pausing on the sidewalk to cross his name out in the Clue Book.

"I'm glad he's not a suspect anymore. I would never have set foot in his arcade again if he'd done something so mean to Katie. But now I can play all the Surf City I want!" George said.

"Although you'll probably have to get in line behind Michael!" Bess said.

Nancy gaped at her friend. "Say that again, Bess."

Bess offered Nancy a perplexed look before repeating, "Um, I said, you'll probably have to get in line behind Michael. Remember how he was bragging about all the high scores he has? I'm sure he'll want to try out Surf City right away."

Nancy started walking again, faster this time, and the other two girls rushed to keep up.

"Where are you going?" George asked as Nancy turned them left onto Main Street.

"I thought of someone else who has a good reason for not wanting Katie to compete today. If the judge from the Beamish Book of World Records was here in town, with no Dance-A-Thon record attempt to watch, she might have time to watch *someone else's* world record attempt. . . ."

Bess and George didn't need any more hints. They knew exactly what Nancy was getting at.

"Hurry!" George said, pointing down a side street. "If we follow the shortcut to Michael's house, we can stay within the five-block radius!"

Nancy, Bess, and George all had the same rule: if they were together, they could travel alone within a five-block radius of one of their houses. Luckily, George lived right in the center of town.

The girls quickened their steps, and when they arrived at their destination a few minutes later, they were greeted by a strange sight.

A *very* strange sight.

Michael was on his front lawn, lying on his back the same way Chocolate Chip did when he wanted his belly scratched. He had one leg up in the air as he wrestled an orange-and-red-striped kneesock over one of his ankles. It looked like he was wearing about thirty socks on that leg already, while his other foot was completely bare. What was going on?

When Michael spotted the girls, he dropped the sock and reached an arm across his chest to a stopwatch lying next to him in the grass. He hit a button on the top of it to pause the sweeping second hand.

"Drat!" he said, making a face. "Thirteen seconds too slow."

Bess put a hand on her hip and peered at Michael. "Um, what exactly are you *doing*?"

He gave a tug and pulled the whole stack from his foot, then jumped up to stand in front of them. He used the jumble of socks in his hand to wipe some sweat from his brow, which made Bess's nose wrinkle.

"I told you I was working on my own world record attempt," Michael said in a very matter-of-fact voice.

George laughed. "What's the record? Goofiest person alive?"

"No," Michael explained. "I'm trying to become the person who can put the most socks on one foot in one minute. The world record holder got to forty-five. I did forty-eight once, but no one was around to record it, and I haven't been able to repeat it since. I know I can, though."

He dropped the mass of socks to the ground. They were all different colors and sizes.

"Oh, wow. That's such a unique . . . er, talent," said George.

It was clear from her tone that she didn't think it was much of a talent at all, but she was very polite, and she added a friendly smile. Michael shrugged. "It's not a career choice or anything. I just needed something I could practice easily at home. This is a way easier record to break than Most Watermelons Smashed with a Head or Largest Collection of Rubber Duckies."

He bent and held up a yellow sock covered in a print of tiny ducks.

"And way less dangerous than Longest Sword

Swallowed," said Nancy, who had paged through the Beamish Book of World Records book a time or two herself, marveling at all the weird and wonderful feats.

"Way, *way* less gross than longest fingernails!" added Bess with a shudder.

"Exactly," said Michael, before plopping back down on the grass. "Sorry, guys, but I need to get back to practicing. Just in case the judge has time to see me after she watches Katie's attempt!" He picked up his stopwatch in one hand and a purple polka-dotted sock in his other.

Nancy pulled out her notebook and scribbled something. "So you haven't heard, then?"

Chapter

6

OUT OF CLUES

Michael had moved the purple sock
too close to his face, and he
wrinkled his nose as he took
a whiff. He tossed it back
onto the ground beside him.
Then he looked at the girls.

"Heard what?" he
asked.

They all studied
Michael for his reaction as

Nancy stated, "Katie's lucky headband has been stolen, and she doesn't think she can attempt the record without it."

Michael gasped. "Oh no! That's terrible."

George nodded. "It is. Although, I guess on the bright side, now the judge will have plenty of time on his or her hands. . . ." But Michael was already shaking his head. "Nope. No way. She's bound to be upset by a change in plans. The last thing anyone wants is to attempt a record in front of a cranky judge."

Michael began pulling apart the giant stack of socks. He paused and looked at the girls. "Besides, I couldn't do that to Katie. Us world record attempters stick together. I wanted us *both* to earn one today. I'd hate to win one *instead* of her."

He piled his socks into his arms and straightened up. "If she's not attempting today, then neither am I."

The girls exchanged glances. It was clear they were all having the same thought: if Michael would only compete if Katie did, that would make him the last person to take her headband.

But now what? They were fresh out of clues . . . again!

The afternoon sun was beating down on the yard, and Michael offered the girls a cold drink while he put his bundle of socks away.

He deposited the pile on a bench in the mudroom, and then they followed him through the dining room and into the kitchen, passing Michael's little sister, Caroline, on the way. She was sitting at the table, which was covered in newspapers and hot-pink glitter. She was so absorbed in her craft project, she didn't even

notice when Bess called out a hello to her.

George elbowed Bess. "That's kind of like you when a new clothing catalog comes in the mail."

Beth smiled and elbowed her cousin back. In the kitchen, Michael handed each girl a tall glass of icy water, which they drank standing up.

As they placed their empty glasses in the sink, Nancy said, "Maybe we should head back to the arcade and see if there have been any developments in the case since we've been gone. It's always possible the headband turned up."

Bess and George agreed. Michael walked them to the door and cast a wistful glance at his sock pile as he wished them luck.

The girls hurried along the sidewalk to Starcade, hoping that they'd return to find Katie happily bopping around the dance mat with her lucky headband keeping her bangs off her face. They spent the short walk comparing some of the funnier world records they had read about (Longest Bumper Car Marathon! World's Largest

Pepperoni Pizza! Most Hot Dogs Eaten in One Minute!).

They held their breath as they entered the arcade, but let it out in a whoosh when they immediately spotted the Dance-A-Thon game sitting quietly in the corner.

Nancy quickly spied Katie by the air hockey tables, deep in conversation with her mother and the arcade owner. Some of the crowd from earlier had thinned out, which wasn't a good sign.

Had everyone given up on Katie?

Well, at least it didn't look like the judge had arrived yet. They still had time to solve this mystery—even if they *were* out of clues.

But just then George leaned in close to the other two girls and whispered, "I think I found another suspect for us to interview."

Chapter 7

THE RIVAL

With her chin, George motioned toward Max Bensen. When Nancy had talked to Deirdre earlier, the budding reporter had mentioned that the current Dance-A-Thon world record holder was visiting from out of town. He planned to watch in person as his record was challenged.

And now he was just coming out of the restroom. He shot a quick look over at Katie and the adults, then spun and turned toward the Skee-Ball machine.

"He definitely looks suspicious," said Bess. "And why would he come all the way here to celebrate someone breaking his record? Very suspicious, if you ask me!"

George and Nancy agreed, and all three girls beelined straight for Max, who had just dropped a token into the Skee-Ball game and was waiting for the small bowling balls to roll to him.

He picked up the first one in his hand and brought his arm back to roll it, only to encounter Nancy's leg.

"Oops, sorry!" he exclaimed. "I should have been paying better attention."

"That's okay," Nancy said, stepping aside. "We didn't mean to get in your way. But now that we have, would you have time for a few questions?"

Max tilted his head and looked at the girls beside him. "Sure. I guess. Do you mind if I play while we talk?"

"Not at all," George replied.

Nancy took out the Clue Book and a pen and waited for Max to send his first ball zooming up the ramp. It landed in the forty-point hole, before bouncing right out and rolling into the gutter.

"Ouch! Tough luck," said Bess.

Max looked embarrassed. "Thanks. This isn't really my game."

"Oh, we know," said George. "Your game is Dance-A-Thon, right? We heard that you're the current world record holder."

Max looked proud. He picked up the next ball and shook out his shoulders. "For the moment, at least!" he said. He tossed a quick glance over his shoulder at Katie, who was still standing at the air hockey tables with her mom.

The Clue Crew followed his eyes.

George said softly, "Yeah. It must be hard to imagine giving up your title."

Max turned his attention back to the game and sent the next ball rocketing up the ramp. This one landed in the fifty-point hole—and bounced right back out. Max made a face.

"This game takes a gentle touch," Nancy said, trying to make Max feel better about his score.

"That's for sure," he agreed. "Now. What were you saying before?"

George repeated herself. "I said, it must be hard to imagine giving up your title."

Max shrugged. "Yes and no. Sure, I love being the titleholder, but to be honest, before Katie came along, I was actually getting a little bored with Dance-A-Thon."

"Really?" asked Bess, incredulous. "How can you get bored with something when you're the best in the world at it?"

Max picked up his next ball and bowled it so softly, it didn't even make it up the ramp. The girls bit their cheeks and tried not to laugh. For all of Max's skills on the dance pad, he really wasn't so good at Skee-Ball. The ball rolled slowly back to him, and he grabbed it with a sigh before answering them.

"If Katie beats me today, I get to try to reclaim the record back from her. I'm excited to have a real opponent again. It's so much more fun when there's someone playing at your level. It forces you to work hard to get even better. I love that!"

The girls exchanged a look.

"So you actually *want* her to steal your record away from you?" Bess asked, a note of disbelief in her voice.

Max nodded. "Well, yeah, actually."

He looked around to make sure no one was eavesdropping. "Katie and I have both been approached by a spokesperson for an energy bar company. They want to sponsor a "boy versus girl" dance-off between the two top Dance-A-Thon players in the world. In fact, I'm here today so we can do our first photo op together. Of course, if she doesn't grab the record from me in the first place . . ."

"All that money goes away?" Nancy filled in when Max trailed off.

He looked embarrassed. "Um, well, not money. They offered to pay us with a lifetime supply of energy bars instead." He paused, before adding, "But they're *really* good!"

He extracted a wrapped bar from the pocket of his jacket. "Here, you guys should try one."

George opened the package and the three girls divided the snack, as Max returned his attention to the Skee-Ball game. This time he rolled his ball with just the right amount of speed. It landed in the ten-point hole.

Max laughed. "Well, at least I'm on the scoreboard. Although I won't be getting any sponsorships to play Skee-Ball, that's for sure."

Nancy, George, and Bess had their mouths too full of the yummy energy bar to do much more than smile in reply.

Max rolled his next few balls with varying

success, while the girls chewed. He picked up his ninth and final one, saying, "Here goes nothing!"

This time, when he stretched his hand behind him to prepare to send the ball rolling, he didn't bump into Nancy's leg. Instead he bumped into a teenage boy carrying a soda.

It was like everything slowed down as the soda arced through the air, headed straight for Bess! She squeaked and tried to move out of the way, but she wasn't nearly fast enough.

The sticky soda landed right on her arms and all over the front of her shirt.

Chapter 8

A BIG MESS

Bess peered down at her favorite pink unicorn T-shirt, now covered in dark, syrupy soft-drink splatters.

"Oh no! It'll be ruined!" she cried.

"I'm so sorry," said both Max and the teen with the drink, at the same time.

"It was an accident," Nancy reassured them. "Don't worry, Bess, we can get it cleaned off."

"I'll grab some paper towels from the bathroom," Max offered.

"I'll help," added the other boy, probably so he wouldn't be stuck with an annoyed-looking Bess.

The boys disappeared, leaving the three girls alone. Bess whimpered softly and tugged her shirt away from her. "It's cold," she whined.

George and Nancy gave her sympathetic looks.

"Help is on the way," Nancy reminded her.

Then George's expression turned even sadder. "We can't catch a break today. Bess is covered in soda, and Max's story really seems to check out. I don't think he took Katie's headband, do you?"

Nancy shook her head and Bess just whimpered again, but when the other two girls looked at her, she shook her head too.

She added, "We're no closer to solving the case, and the judge could arrive at any minute now. I can't believe Katie won't get to dance."

"No way am I accepting that," said Nancy

firmly. "We're the best junior detectives in River Heights. We *will* find a way to solve this before it's time for the attempt."

Bess craned her neck in the direction of the bathrooms. "What's taking those boys so long? Some of the soda got on my neck, and now it's dripping down my belly. It feels really gross!"

George stood on tiptoes to look for them, but Nancy suddenly had a better idea. "The washcloths in Katie's bag! I'm sure she won't mind if we borrow a few, and they'll do a way better job than the paper towels from the bathroom. I'll go grab them."

She raced over to the pinball machine. Katie's duffel was still tucked underneath it, just where the Clue Crew had returned it after their examination. It was still unzipped and messy. Nancy lugged the whole thing over to the Skee-Ball machines.

Plopping it on the floor, she reached inside for the soft washcloths. She pulled two out and handed them to Bess, who immediately began using one to blot at her shirt and the other to wipe off her sticky belly. George giggled to see her friend rubbing both cloths in opposite circles.

"That's like when I try to rub my stomach and pat my head at the same time," she said, still giggling.

Bess gave her cousin a look.

After a few seconds, Bess stopped and tucked her chin down to peer at the front of her shirt.

"Do you think this is helping?" she asked.

Nancy and George both grimaced. If anything, Bess had made things worse. Her shirt definitely needed a washing machine.

"I'm sure Hannah will be able to help, Bess," Nancy said.

Hannah was Nancy's housekeeper, and she knew how to do, well, everything. "She always gets the grass marks out of my jeans after I roll around in the yard with Chocolate Chip," she added. Nancy hoped her words would cheer up her friend, but Bess still looked miserable. "This is my favorite shirt."

George leaned in. "I can see why. I may not be the biggest fan of pink myself, but the rhinestone on the unicorn's horn is really cool. It makes it look 3-D!"

Bess's nose went crinkly as she scrunched up her face. "This shirt doesn't have rhinestones, George."

George gave her cousin an *Are you crazy?* look and said, "I may not be super girly, but I'm pretty sure I know a rhinestone when I see one." She pointed at Bess's shirt. "Voilà!"

Bess pulled the shirt away from her skin and examined the unicorn on its front. "But . . . but that wasn't there before. Of all people, I would know if my shirt was BeDazzled! That would have made it my *extra* favorite."

Then she squinted even closer. "And wait! There's pink glitter, too. Girls, I think we have another mystery to solve."

Nancy looked puzzled, and so did her friends, but after a second, she gasped and her expression became thoughtful. Then she asked, "Bess, what's Katie wearing today?"

River Heights's resident fashionista was ready with an immediate response: "Black leggings, a hot-pink tutu, and a shirt that says 'girl power.' Topped off with those hot-pink streaks in her hair—I can't wait until I'm old enough to ask Mom for some of those. They're the coolest!"

George rolled her eyes, but Nancy wasn't done asking questions. "Except she wasn't wearing any glitter anywhere, right? Or rhinestones?"

Bess shook her head slowly. "Definitely not."

Nancy looked from Katie's duffel to the wash-cloth in Bess's hands. When she shook the cloth, some pink glitter fluttered to the ground.

Then she smiled serenely. "Clue Crew? I think I just solved *both* mysteries."

Clue Crew—and
YOU!

Can you solve the mystery of the missing head-band? Write your answers on a sheet of paper. Or just turn the page to find out!

1. Nancy, Bess, and George came up with three suspects. Can you think of more? Grab a sheet of paper and write down your suspects.

2. Who do you think has the missing headband? Write it down on a sheet of paper.

3. What clues helped you solve this mystery? Write them down on a piece of paper.

Chapter 9

ALL THAT GLITTERS

George and Bess stared at Nancy, waiting for her to explain what she'd meant when she said she'd just solved both mysteries. Before they could ask, the two boys returned with fistfuls of napkins in their hands.

Max said, "The paper towel dispenser in the bathroom was empty, so we had to detour to the snack bar. Here you go."

Bess waved them off. "Thanks, but we're all set."

She was eager to hear Nancy's theory. Her shirt could wait! Max and the other boy looked confused, but they shrugged and set the napkins next to Bess.

"They're there if you need them. We're going to play Monaco Racetrack," Max told them.

Bess and George gave distracted thanks and waves as the boys left.

"What do you mean, you solved both mysteries?" George asked, turning back to Nancy.

Nancy gave them a secret smile. "It's just a hunch . . . but I think I'm right. We need to get back to Michael's house."

The cousins exchanged confused looks.

"But we already ruled out Michael as a suspect!" Bess protested.

Nancy's smile grew even bigger. "We did. But I'm not interested in talking to Michael this time."

Still baffled, Bess and George trailed Nancy out of the arcade. They were barely to the corner, though, when a small cluster of adults blocked their path. They could see that the mayor of River Heights was part of the group.

As they drew closer, the three girls could tell that everyone was listening to a woman holding a clipboard and wearing a navy-blue business suit. Over her shoulder was a soft-sided briefcase embroidered with the words BEAMISH BOOK OF WORLD RECORDS.

"That must be the judge!" Bess said in a hushed voice.

The girls moved aside to let the group pass. They watched carefully as everyone paused outside the entrance to the arcade. Sure enough, the mayor reached over and opened the door, ushering the others inside.

"Hurry! There's no time to waste!" Nancy yelled, tucking her notebook into her pocket and picking up her pace to a run. George and Bess did the same.

They careened around the corner and nearly crashed right into Michael and Caroline. All five kids spilled onto the concrete, but luckily, no one was hurt.

"Where's the fire?" asked Michael.

"Actually . . . we were . . . coming to see . . . you," George said through huffs and puffs as she collected her breath after running so hard.

"Me?" asked Michael.

But Nancy was shaking her head. "Nope. Not you. Actually, we were coming to see your sister."

Bess and George swiveled their necks to stare at Nancy.

Caroline squeaked, "You were?" in a small voice.

Nancy smiled reassuringly. "Yes, and we have no time to waste, because the world record judge just arrived. If we don't act fast, Katie might tell her she can't compete today!"

"What does that have to do with my sister?" Michael asked.

Nancy turned to Caroline, who was still sitting on the sidewalk, looking alarmed. "Caroline? Is there any chance you have Katie's lucky headband in your bag?"

Everyone gaped at the little girl, who immediately pulled her purse to her. It was decorated with hot-pink glitter swirls, and row after row of tiny rhinestones dotted the edges. Bess and George both gasped when they spotted the embellishments.

"Rhinestones!" whispered Bess.

"Glitter," whispered George.

Nancy held up the washcloth she still carried in her hand.

"A perfect match," she added.

Caroline reached inside and extracted a stretchy fabric headband, which was covered in hot-pink glitter and rhinestone accents.

"Sure. It's right here," she said. "I was just bringing it back to Katie before she went for the world record."

Bess couldn't contain her groan. "We've been all over town looking for that. Katie's really upset it went missing!"

Caroline bit her bottom lip and looked like she might cry. "She is? I thought for sure I'd get it back to her before she even noticed, but the glue was taking forever to dry and I wanted to make extra sure the rhinestones wouldn't fall off while she danced. It took way longer than I expected."

Michael stared at his sister. "Caroline! You should have known better."

"But Nancy and Bess were so excited about my designs, and then I saw Katie put away her plain-as-could-be headband and I thought maybe I could surprise her for her special day. I didn't mean to cause any problems!" Caroline looked so small and upset that none of the other kids had the heart to lecture her.

Instead Bess said, "It really does look great. And I'll bet Katie will love it. Let's hurry and get it to her before it's too late!"

Caroline still looked glum at how badly her surprise had backfired, but she scrambled to her feet and joined the others as they raced back to the arcade.

Chapter 10

GO, KATIE!

"I hope Katie hasn't had a chance to cancel her attempt yet!" Nancy said as she held the door open for the others to jostle inside.

They all went straight to the Dance-A-Thon game, where they could see Katie standing amid a small circle of people, including the judge and the mayor of River Heights.

Katie was gesturing, and from the expression on her face, it was clear she was telling the judge she couldn't dance that afternoon.

"Wait!" called Bess, George, and Nancy.

Their three voices combined to rise above the dings and whistles and music of the noisy arcade. Katie peered over the judge's shoulder at the members of the Clue Crew. Nancy held the BeDazzled headband above her, and Katie's eyes widened. Her hand went to her mouth.

The girls stopped right in front of her, and Nancy offered Katie the headband. Michael and Caroline pushed in behind them.

"Is that my headband?" Katie cried. "Who— where did you—" She paused and took a breath. "*How* did you find it?"

Bess linked arms with Nancy and George. "A little good old-fashioned detective work," she said with a giant grin.

Katie grinned too. "I'm so happy I had you guys in my corner today."

The girls shrugged modestly, then explained to the dancer what had happened.

Katie glanced down at the headband in her hand and examined it closely. "Wow! This is a work of art now. Who did you say did this?"

Michael gently pushed his sister to the front. "She did."

Caroline kept her eyes on the ground, avoiding Katie's, as she said, "I'm really sorry. I was only trying to surprise you and give you something to help cheer you on."

Katie waited for Caroline to sneak a peek up at her, and then she smiled. "I truly love it. I'll feel extra sparkly as I fly across the dance floor."

Caroline swallowed. "You're—you're not mad?"

Katie shook her head. "I wish you'd told someone about your special plan, but I understand why you wanted to keep it a surprise. If there's one thing I learned early on—when I was trying to master Dance-A-Thon—it's that everyone messes up. That's why it's great that games come with a reset button. I think life should too."

Caroline's answering smile was as sparkly as Katie's glitter-ific new headband, especially after Katie hugged her.

The judge, who'd been standing just behind

Katie as the whole scene went down, cleared her throat. "Well, I, for one, certainly hope you don't need that reset button today, Katie. I'll be cheering hard for your perfect score. But we should get started or I won't have time to see your triumphant finish before my train leaves to go back to the city."

Katie squared her shoulders and grinned. "Okay. Let's do this thing!"

She smoothed back her bangs and slipped the lucky headband into place while the arcade made an announcement on their loudspeaker. A crowd quickly formed around the Dance-A-Thon game.

Katie stood in the center of the electronic pad. The rhinestones on her headband flashed under the pulsing lights. She took a deep breath and gave a thumbs-up to her mom, who released a token into the game. It dropped and the screen lit up. Katie winked at the audience as the music kicked in.

"Go, Katie! Go, Katie!" the crowd chanted, no one more enthusiastically than Nancy, Bess, and George.

Well, it's possible Caroline was just a smidge louder.

The score climbed higher and Katie's feet looked like they weren't even attached to her body as they twirled left, right, back, and left again. She spun and shimmied her hips in time to the music, never taking her eyes off the screen's instructions.

After several songs, she finally missed a step and the screen flashed GAME OVER.

The whole arcade hushed and turned to the judge. Smiling at the crowd, then at Katie, she said, "I'm proud to proclaim we have a new world record holder: Ms. Katie McCabe. Congratulations!"

Nancy, George, and Bess joined right in the celebration with everyone else. Michael slipped away to speak to the judge as she put her clipboard into her shoulder bag. Nancy noticed the judge peek at her watch and then nod. Michael's face lit up with a grin. It looked like he'd get to attempt his record as well!

Nancy turned to face her friends. "It's too bad there isn't a world record for solving mysteries."

"It wouldn't even be a contest," added Bess.

George nodded. "Hardly even fair for anyone else attempting it."

The girls smiled at one another. "We don't need a certificate to tell us what we already know," said Nancy.

"The Clue Crew rules!" all three girls shouted together.

Test your detective skills with even more Clue Book mysteries:

Nancy Drew Clue Book #9: Springtime Crime

"Today spring finally feels like spring!" eight-year-old Nancy Drew declared.

It was Friday afternoon and the first mild day of the year. After months of woolly hats, warm scarves, and puffy parkas, Nancy and her two best friends were wearing spring jackets in ice-cream colors.

"It's starting to look like spring too!" Bess Marvin pointed out. "Look at all the pretty flowers."

"Not just flowers, Bess," George said. "Flower sculptures!"

Nancy took a whiff of the awesome-smelling

statues and sculptures made from fresh flowers. The temperature-controlled greenhouse they stood inside was the perfect place for the first annual River Heights Flower Sculpture Show.

"Why are all the flowers pink and white?" Bess wondered. "And round and puffy like ice-skate pom-poms?"

"They're peonies," Nancy replied. "That's the official flower of the show. All the sculptors were told to work with them this year."

"More like pee-*yew*-nees," George said with a frown. "Our next-door neighbors, the Baxters, grow so many that they hang over the fence into our yard!"

"Peonies are so pretty, George," Nancy said. "Why don't you like them?"

"Because bees like them too!" George complained.

Nancy, Bess, and George strolled through the greenhouse. The flower show was on Sunday but people were welcome to watch the sculptors put the finishing touches on their sculptures.

"I like that one best!" Bess said, pointing

to a peony sculpture of a high-heeled shoe.

"No way." George shook her head. "The peony robot is the best."

"High-heeled shoe? Robot?" Nancy teased. "Are you sure you're related?"

Bess and George traded smiles. Not only did the two cousins look different—Bess had blond hair and blue eyes, while George had dark hair and eyes—they liked different things too. Bess loved girly-girl clothes and accessories. George loved accessories too—as long as they went with her computer and electronic gadgets.

"If you were making a flower sculpture, Nancy," Bess asked, "what would it be of?"

"My clue book!" Nancy replied right away.

Bess and George nodded their approval. The three friends were the Clue Crew, the best kid detectives in River Heights. To help solve their mysteries, Nancy used a clue book to write down their thoughts, clues, and suspects.

"These sculptures are totally neat," George admitted, "but the best part of the show on Sunday will be seeing—"

"Miss LaLa!" Bess cut in. "I still can't believe our favorite singer will be the star of the flower sculpture show on Sunday!"

"I already met Miss LaLa," George said. "My mom catered her after-concert party here in River Heights a year ago. Did I ever tell you that?"

"About a hundred times, George," Bess groaned. "You told us she dressed up like a caterpillar inside a cocoon."

Nancy giggled. Miss LaLa was known for her beautiful violet eyes—and her wild costumes!

"I heard that Miss LaLa will wear a huge hat to the flower show," Nancy said excitedly, "totally covered in peonies!"

"Peonies again?" George sighed. "I hope there are no bees in her bonnet."

"Or in that flower cupcake," Bess declared.

Nancy looked to see where Bess was pointing. She smiled when she saw a giant white cupcake made of peonies.

Standing on a ladder while sticking a pink

peony onto the top was a kid the girls recognized at once.

"Hey, it's Benjamin Bing," Nancy said.

"It's him, all right," George agreed. "Who else would sculpt a giant cupcake?"

Ben's parents owned a health food and flower store on Main Street called Bing's Buds and Bran.

"Is it true that no sweets are allowed in Ben's house?" Bess whispered. "Only food from his parents' healthy store?"

Nancy nodded yes. "No wonder Ben likes to sculpt what he can't eat," she said. "Cookies, cakes, cupcakes—"

"Don't forget doughnuts," Ben said, climbing down from the ladder. "I sculpt those, too."

Nancy was embarrassed that Ben had heard them talking about him. "We were also saying how awesome your flower cupcake is, Ben," she said quickly.

"Yeah," George agreed. "It looks like the cupcakes my mom just put on the windowsill to cool."

Ben's eyes grew wide. "Cupcakes?"

"My mom's a caterer," George explained. "She has a special catering kitchen in a trailer behind our house."

"Buttercream frosting f ? Marshmallow?" Ben demanded to know. "Do the cupcakes have sprinkles?"

Nancy tried to change the subject. "How will you keep your flowers fresh until Sunday, Ben?" she blurted.

"Hair spray," Ben said matter-of-factly.

"Hair spray?" Bess asked, surprised. "For flowers?"

"Watch and learn," Ben said. He pulled out an aerosol can and held it a few inches from the fluffy white peonies. Then Ben turned to the girls, spraying as he explained. "Hair spray isn't just for hairstyles anymore. One good spritz will keep your flowers from wilting and even keep the dust off!"

Nancy, Bess, and George stared open-mouthed at Ben's sculpture as he kept spraying and talking. Something . . . was not . . . right. . . .

"Not only that," Ben went on, "clear hair spray will keep flowers nice and firm—"

"Um . . . Ben?" Nancy interrupted.

George formed a T with her hands. "Time out for a second."

"Why?" Ben asked, still spraying away.

"Since when is clear hair spray brown?" Bess asked.

"Huh?" Ben said. He turned to look at his sculpture and gasped. A whole side of his snowy-white cupcake was now brown!

Ben stopped spraying at once. He looked at the can and began to wail. "Arrrgh! This isn't hair spray. It's brown hair dye!"

"It's okay, Ben," Nancy said gently. "Just pluck out the brown ones and replace them with white ones."

"I can't!" Ben cried, pointing to his sculpture. "These are the last peonies from my parents' greenhouse!"

The girls left Ben pacing nervously by his sculpture. Nancy felt bad for him and wanted to help. But how?

"Maybe he could spray-paint them white," George suggested.

"I don't think that would look very good. What about . . ." Bess trailed off mid-thought.

"I may have an idea!" Nancy squeaked.

The three of them had stopped in front of a giant poodle sculpture made of snow-white peonies. In River Heights there was only one sculptor famous for his peony poodles. He was from France and his name was Monsieur Pierre.

"If Pierre uses peonies for his sculptures," Nancy said hopefully, "maybe he has some extras for Ben."

Bess nodded her approval. "Let's ask him!"

But where was Monsieur Pierre? Nancy was about to ask another sculptor, when they heard voices. Angry voices coming from behind the peony poodle.

The girls peeked around the sculpture to see Monsieur Pierre arguing with Mayor Strong.

"I was told I'd be the star of the flower show on Sunday," Pierre said. "How dare you ask Miss LuLu instead?"

"It's 'LaLa,' and we're lucky she'll be singing at the flower show," Mayor Strong said. "Her white peony hat came all the way from Paris, you know."

"Well, so did I!" Pierre scoffed. "And my two poodles, Céline and Celeste!"

Nancy had heard the names Céline and Celeste before. They were Pierre's standard poodles and the models for his sculptures.

"This isn't a good time, you guys," Nancy whispered. "Let's ask another sculptor for peonies."

But as the girls turned to leave . . .

"Girls!" a hushed voice said. "May I speak with you?"

Nancy's eyes widened at the sight of the woman standing behind them. She wore a black trench coat with huge padded shoulders, dark cat-eye sunglasses, and fire-engine-red lipstick. Her blond hair was tied in a low bun, and she was holding a large brown paper shopping bag.

"Um . . . do we know you?" Nancy asked.

"I think you do," the woman said. She

lowered her sunglasses to reveal the deepest violet-blue eyes.

Nancy, Bess, and George gasped. Only one person in the world had eyes like that. It was—

"Miss LaLa!" Nancy cried. "Omigosh!"

NANCY DREW AND THE CLUE CREW®
Test your detective skills with more Clue Crew cases!

Visit NancyDrew.com for the inside scoop!

From Aladdin · KIDS.SimonandSchuster.com

FOLLOW THE TRAIL AND SOLVE MYSTERIES WITH FRANK AND JOE!

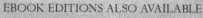

FUR AND FUN FLY AT THE ANIMAL INN—
A SPA AND HOTEL FOR PETS!

A Furry Fiasco

Treasure Hunt

The Bow-wow Bus